A Note to Parents

You can help your Level 3 reader.

★ Keep up the habit of reading aloud with your older child. For many years, your child's listening comprehension will be greater than his or her ability to read alone.

★ Make reading with your child interactive. Try taking turns—you read one page, your child reads the next. Sit side by side.

★ Let your child read aloud the main character's part, while you read the other parts. This technique will help improve your child's comprehension, expression, and fluency.

Extend and enhance the reading experience.

★ Build background knowledge by relating this book to other books your child has read.

★ Find new books on topics your child likes, such as space travel or wild animals. Choose different kinds of books, including poetry, biography, and fiction.

★ Visit a museum, zoo, or theater to enrich current interests and discover new ones.

★ Be a role model. Let your child see you reading. Share your enjoyment by reading aloud fantastic phrases or humorous tidbits.

★ As your child becomes a fluent reader and prefers to read alone, provide a quiet, comfortable reading corner.

Most of all, enjoy your reading time together!

—**Bernice Cullinan, Ph.D.,**
Professor of Reading, New York University

To Chris
—SJB

To Pat
—RH

Many thanks to Scott Schliebe of the U.S. Fish and
Wildlife Service for reviewing the text and
artwork for this book.

Reader's Digest Children's Books
Reader's Digest Road, Pleasantville, NY 10570-7000
Copyright © 2000 Reader's Digest Children's Publishing, Inc.
All rights reserved. Reader's Digest Children's Books and All-Star Readers are
trademarks and Reader's Digest is a registered trademark
of The Reader's Digest Association, Inc.
Printed in Hong Kong
10 9 8 7 6 5 4 3 2 1

Library of Congress Cataloging-in-Publication Data is available.

Polar Bear
Growing Up in the Icy North

by Sarah Jane Brian
illustrated by Robert Hynes

3
All-Star Readers™
Reader's Digest Children's Books™
Pleasantville, New York • Montréal, Québec

Deep inside a snow den, a baby polar bear opens her eyes.

Not much light comes through the snow roof. The cub can just see the huge shape of her mother. Her brother is a tiny furry ball. She hears the wind howl and groan outside.

It is winter in the far north.

The cub snuggles between her mother's big warm paws. She drinks her mother's milk and plays with her brother. They dig a new tunnel to play in.

Soon it is spring. The cub watches her mother crawl up to scratch at the roof of snow. Cold air rushes into the den. The mother bear sniffs the air.

The next day, she pokes her head out. What is going on outside? The cub can't see anything.

Days later, the mother climbs up and out of the den. She waits to make sure it is safe. Finally, the cub hears her mother call, Chuff! Chuff! That means, "Come to me!"

Outside, everything is scary and
new. Hills of snow slope down to an icy
black sea. Mountains of rock rise high into
the sky.

The mother bear licks her babies' faces.
After a while, the cub is not so afraid.
She jumps on her brother and they
roll in the snow. They slide down a hill on
their backsides.

Each day the baby bears come out to play. They stay near the safe den.

The mother bear is getting hungry. She has not eaten in six months. One day, she decides to go hunting. Chuff! Chuff! The cub and her brother follow their mother to the sea.

They will never return to their den again.

The cub sees interesting new animals by the water. A small white fox runs around the polar bear family.

A huge walrus rests on the ice. The bears stay away from the walrus. It could hurt the cubs with its sharp tusks.

The mother bear finds a hole in the ice. The cub knows to stay quiet as her mother lies down to wait.

Soon a seal comes up to breathe. In a flash, the bear's long sharp claws grab the seal and flip it out of the water.

The cub licks at the seal, but this food is not for her.

The mother bear quickly eats. Then she rolls in the snow to clean off. The cub rolls, too. Her brother licks some snow from between his toes.

The mother bear leads the way across the ice. Traveling for miles, the bears look for food.

When their mother jumps into the cold water, the baby bears swim behind. Sometimes they jump between big chunks of ice.

In summer, most of the ice melts.
The sun stays in the sky all day and all
night. Flowers bloom and birds come
to stay.

The cub is curious about everything.
She plays with plants and pokes at a nest.
The mother bear sleeps in the sun.
Without ice, it is hard to hunt.

Soon the weather starts getting colder. Flowers die and bushes change color.

The cub is growing fast. Every day she drinks milk and gets stronger. She already weighs 130 pounds.

When the ice returns, the bears
go hunting again. One day they see a
big male bear.

The cub stands on her back legs to get
a better look. She can see that her
mother is nervous. This stranger might
hurt the cubs!

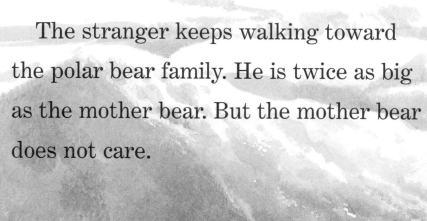

The stranger keeps walking toward
the polar bear family. He is twice as big
as the mother bear. But the mother bear
does not care.

She runs at the stranger as fast as she can. Her sharp teeth and fierce noises scare the stranger away.

Each day is colder and colder. But the polar bears do not dig a den.

One day a bad storm comes.

The cub curls up with her mother and brother. Falling snow makes a blanket to keep them warm.

During the long winter, the sun
never rises. But the mother bear keeps
hunting. The cub watches and learns. By
springtime, she wants to hunt, too.

One day the cub sees a seal asleep
on the ice. Slowly, slowly, she crawls
toward the seal.

Splash! The seal dives into an ice hole.

The cub keeps trying to hunt.
Every day she learns more. In the fall,
she wanders off by herself. It is the cub's
first time alone! She explores for a while
and then returns.

Her mother touches noses to welcome
the cub back.

When the ice starts to freeze this year, the cub is almost as big as her mother.

One day the young bear smells a hole in the ice. She kneels down, watching and waiting.

The cub waits an hour. Then a seal swims up. The seal can't see the white bear on the white ice.

Wham! The cub grabs the seal and slams it down.

Now the cub leaves to hunt more often. She stays away longer.

Sometimes she play-fights with her brother. The young bears are practicing. When they live on their own, they will have to defend themselves.

But for now, the cubs never wander too far from their mother. She still protects them and gives them food.

In spring, the cub comes back from a trip. She spots her mother resting on the ice and walks over to touch noses.

But something has changed.

Instead of touching noses, her mother
growls. She runs at the cub and pushes
with her head.

The mother bear is telling her to
go away!

The cub tries to come back. Again and again, she is chased away. The mother bear chases off her son, too. It is time for the young bears to live on their own.

At last the cub sets out across the cold ice. Her brother comes along with her.

After a while, their mother will mate again and have new cubs.

The cub does not stay with her brother for long. She is almost an adult now. Adult bears travel and hunt alone.

She walks and swims for hundreds of miles. When winter comes, she braves the storms by herself.

When she is five years old, the young bear is fully grown. She meets a male bear and mates with him.

That fall, she eats and eats. She gains 500 pounds!

When she finds a quiet snow bank, the polar bear begins to dig a cozy den.

Soon she has a new family. Now it is her turn to teach her cubs the ways of the icy north.

More About Polar Bears...

Polar bears live in Canada, Alaska, and Russia. Some have even been spotted near the North Pole! Many bears live where the ice never melts. Unlike the animals in this book, they stay on the ice and never see land... A newborn polar bear is about the size of a kitten. Two grown-up male bears can weigh as much as a small car... A polar bear's thick fur looks white, but each hair is actually clear. Underneath, the bear's skin is black from nose to toes. Even its tongue is black! When sunlight shines through the clear fur, the dark skin holds in heat.

Check Your Knowledge of Polar Bears!

Place an All-Star sticker on the line under **T** *if the answer is true and under* **F** *if the answer is false.*

	T	F
1. A polar bear's skin is black.	_____	_____
2. Baby polar bears live in rock caves.	_____	_____
3. A mother bear will defend her cubs against a large bear.	_____	_____
4. A baby cub drinks its mother's milk.	_____	_____
5. All polar bears spend some time on land.	_____	_____
6. A cub learns to hunt by watching its mother.	_____	_____
7. Adult bears travel and hunt in packs.	_____	_____
8. Bear cubs like to play in the snow.	_____	_____
9. Polar bears hunt by waiting near an ice hole.	_____	_____

Answers: 1-T; 2-F; 3-T; 4-T; 5-F; 6-T; 7-F; 8-T; 9-T